Published by Get You Visible Publishing www.getyouvisible.com

Illustrated by Gina Daws.

ISBN # print version: 978-1-989848-14-2
ISBN# Ebook version: 978-1-989848-15-9

Buster
the
Bridger Mountain Bear

By Wayne Edwards
Illustrated By Gina Daws

MEET THE ANIMALS OF BRIDGER MOUNTAIN

BILLY BOB BOBCAT
Bobcats are smaller than Cougars, but bigger than house cats.
Billy Bob has a short "bob" tail, and he is scrappy and feisty.

WILMA THE WHITE-TAILED DEER
Wilma is shy and nervous; she is also very quick and fast.
She is nice and all the animals like her…She is Gabby Gopher's best friend.

BRUTUS BADGER
Brutus is always in a bad mood and is so crabby that he doesn't have many friends on Bridger Mountain.
Badgers are nocturnal. Do you know what nocturnal means? You're right! It means they sleep during the day
and are awake at night.

MEET THE ANIMALS OF BRIDGER MOUNTAIN

GABRIELLE "GABBY" GOPHER

Gabby likes to gossip. That means she's nosey and talks about the other animals.

Gabby knows all the animals on Bridger Mountain, and is always willing to help any animal in need.

BUSTER THE BEAR

Buster is a black bear. Did you know some black bears are brown?

Buster is friendly and curious.

He likes to eat huckleberries, insects and honey.

MORTIMER "MORT" MOOSE

Mort has really large horns.

He is friendly, but awkward. Do you know what awkward means?

You're right again! It means he is clumsy.

MEET THE ANIMALS OF BRIDGER MOUNTAIN

OLIVER WENDELL OWL, III
Oliver is very old and sage. Do you know what sage means? You're right! It means he is smart and wise. If any animal has a problem, they come to Oliver for advice on how to solve it.

CATERINA "CAT" COUGAR
Cat is a Mountain Cougar. Cougars are sometimes called Mountain Lions. Cat has a long tail and moves so quietly and swiftly that she is seldom seen.

ERNESTO "ERNIE" ELK
Ernie is regal. Do you know what regal means? You are so smart! Yes, it means he is noble and proud. Ernie has really big horns that are called antlers.

MEET THE ANIMALS OF BRIDGER MOUNTAIN

FRANCESCA "FRANNIE" FOX
Did you know that foxes are so sneaky they can steal eggs out of a henhouse without the chickens even knowing they were there?
Frannie will be hiding on every page. Do you think you can find her?

BEAVIS "BUCKY" BEAVER
Beavers use their big, sharp teeth to cut down trees to make a lodge or fort in a creek or river.
Bucky is the best wood chopper on all of Bridger Creek.

SAVANNAH SKUNK
Savannah is sweet and all the animals like her.
But do you know why no one wants to get very close to her? You guessed it! Skunks can be stinky, so it's best to keep your distance.

Gabby Gopher lived on Bridger Mountain.
She liked waking up to the early morning sunshine.

Gabby followed the cries for help to the meadow. She was surprised to find Buster the Bear with his head stuck in a log.

"Stay CALM, Buster. I'll go get HELP!" said Gabby.

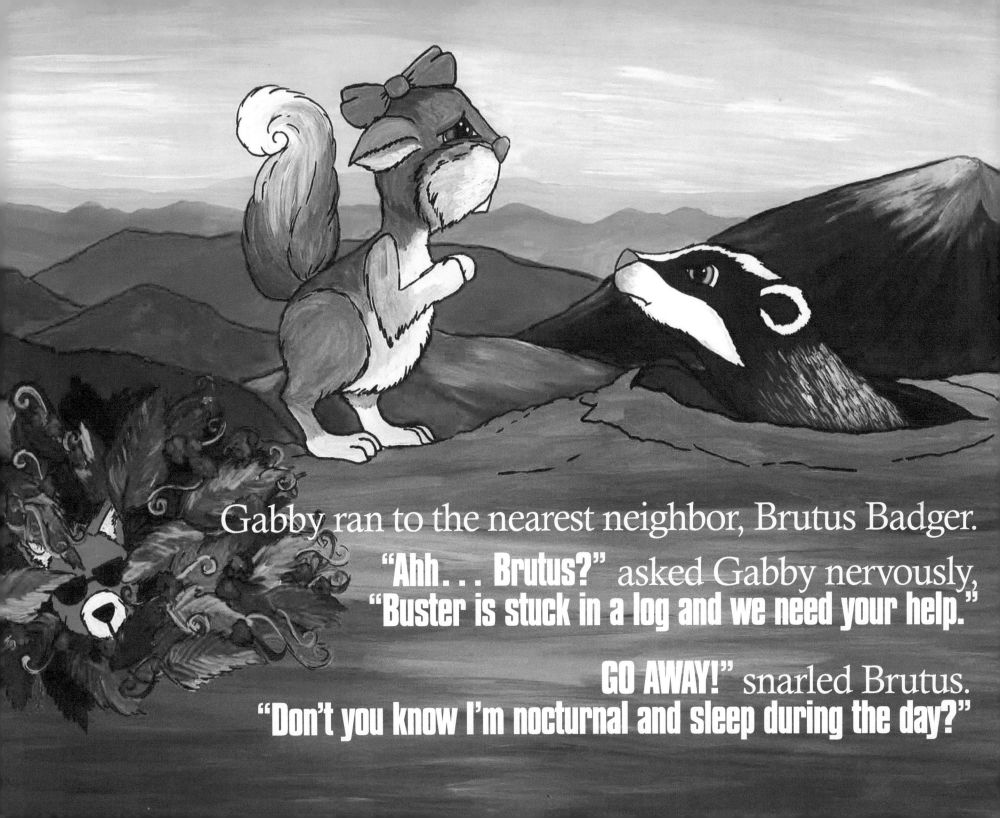

Gabby ran to the nearest neighbor, Brutus Badger.

"Ahh... Brutus?" asked Gabby nervously,
"Buster is stuck in a log and we need your help."

GO AWAY!" snarled Brutus.
"Don't you know I'm nocturnal and sleep during the day?"

With no help from Brutus,
Gabby ran to find her best friend, Wilma.

"Buster is stuck in a log and I need to hitch a ride!
We must find Caterina Cougar and Billy Bob Bobcat!"

Buster the Bear page 5

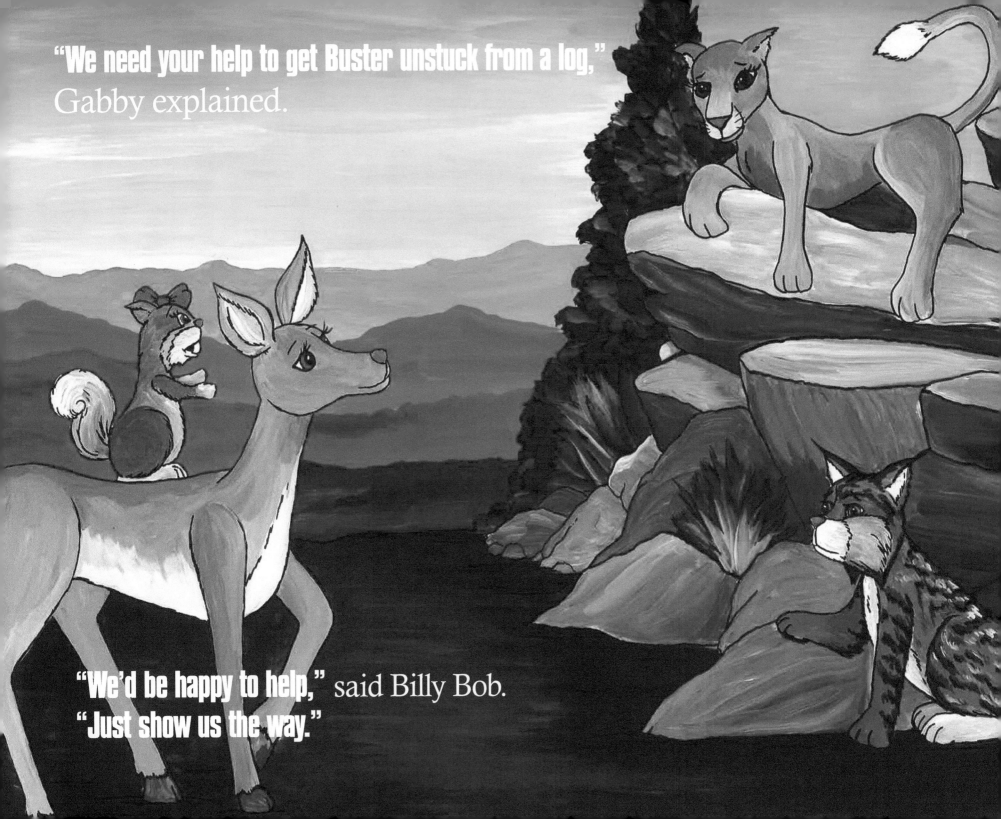

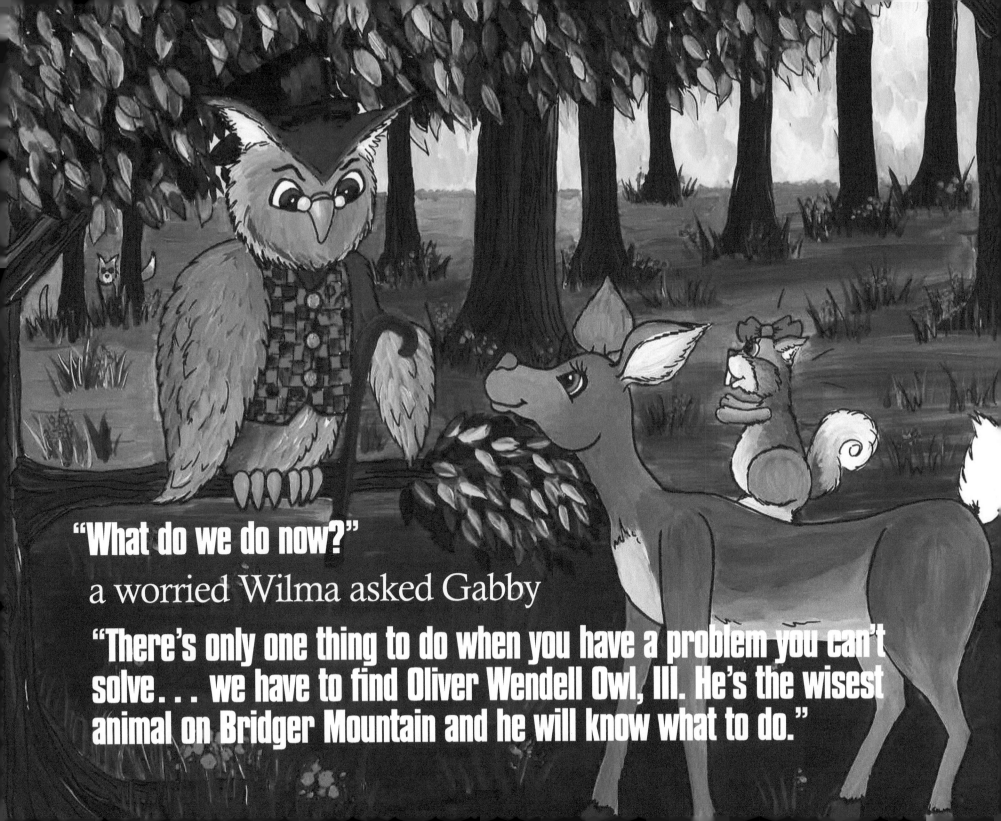

"What do we do now?"

a worried Wilma asked Gabby

"There's only one thing to do when you have a problem you can't solve. . . . we have to find Oliver Wendell Owl, III. He's the wisest animal on Bridger Mountain and he will know what to do."

"**What's that smell?**" barked Oliver Owl.
"**Oh, that's just Savannah the Skunk—she came to help,**" Gabby explained.

"**Well, move her down wind. How am I supposed to solve this problem when it's too stinky to even think?**" grumbled Oliver.

"**You know what to do to get Buster unstuck, don't you Mr. Owl?**" Gabby asked anxiously.

"**Hmm... hmm, yes, that should do the trick,**" mumbled Oliver Owl as he looked at Buster's head stuck in the log. "**We need to get Buster and this log down to Bucky Beaver's lodge on Bridger Creek.**"

"I still don't how we're going to get Buster and this log all the way down to Bridger Creek," said a puzzled Billy Bob.

"Just hold your horses," ordered Oliver Owl. "I'm about to show you. Mort and Ernie… you guys will put your horns down on the ground next to the log......."

"I GET IT!! I GET IT!!" squealed Gabby. "The rest of us push Buster and the log onto their horns, and Mort and Ernie will carry them down to Bridger Creek!"

"You are so wise, Mr. Owl," said Caterina Cougar.
"I could have figured that out," muttered Brutus. "Badgers are no dummies, you know!"

"You did it! You did it!"
screeched Gabby as Mort and Ernie strained to lift Buster and the log above their heads.

"MARCH.. ONE.. TWO.. THREE. . .MARCH!"

"**Hmm.. hmm,**" said Bucky. "**This will be a tricky job cutting this log off of Buster's neck.**"
"**But you can do it, can't you Bucky?**" asked Gabby, worriedly.

"**This is no job for your ordinary beaver,**" said Bucky.
"**You were smart to come to a wood-cutting professional like me!**"

Bucky began to carefully whittle away on the log.

"Ma?" asked Bucky. "This will take awhile—can you make snacks for everybody?"

Bucky went back to work...CUTTING and CHOMPING, CHOMPING and CUTTING.

Everyone else took a nap.

"Everybody WAKE UP!!" shouted Bucky. "I'm almost done!"

"But you haven't cut all the way through the log yet," said Gabby. "Buster is still stuck!"
"Not for long, he isn't!" said Bucky, puffing out his chest

"STAND BACK!" he ordered. Bucky then raised his
mighty tail paddle HIGH above the log and….

"Buster, you're free!" hollered Gabby as the animals gathered around the happy bear to give him hugs.

"Pee-eww!" said Oliver, glaring down at Savannah.

"So sorry, so sorry," apologized the mother skunk. **"I got so excited I flipped my tail by mistake!"**

"Oh my gosh, how can I ever thank you all for getting me unstuck?"
The animals of Bridger Mountain are the best, that's for sure."

"Shucks, it weren't nothin'," said Mortimer M
"Always happy to give a helping horn."

AND NO ONE WAS HAPPIER ABOUT
GOING HOME THAN BUSTER
THE BRIDGER MOUNTAIN BEAR!!

CPSIA information can be obtained
at www.ICGtesting.com
Printed in the USA
BVHW091204251121
622511BV00003B/38